LOVE AND OTHER

BROKEN THINGS

Deidrea DeWitt

ISBN Paperback:
#978-1-7342866-4-9

Cover design by nskvsky

For more works by the author, please visit
www.deidreadewitt.com

To my idol.

To my God.

To my composition.

PART ONE:

LOVE AND OTHER

BROKEN THINGS

Being deeply loved by someone

gives you strength,

while loving someone deeply

gives you courage.

- **Lao Tzu**

VOICE

It started with your voice.

The way each note in your vocal chords
hummed, soothing the coarse and battered
places in my heart that had given up on
healing. Each one of your words weaved
through my veins, strengthening the frayed
and torn threads that were barely tied
together.

You had a melody to you.
A tune I had never heard before.

You were the major key that lifted my spirit
in the morning; and you were the minor key
that made my soul burn at night.

It was your voice - your rich, powerful voice

that led me to love you. Your words and sounds penetrated the places in my soul that were silent and lifeless. Your voice was the replacement for mine - a voice that had been too broken to speak.

When you spoke, I drank in every word, letting them drip down my throat until I was filled with you.

And I drank...
until the only thing I thirsted for was you.

REPLAY

I was addicted to your melody.

I played -

and replayed -

your voice,

your rhythms,

the harmonies God had blended together

to make you.

Light and darkness wove together in each of

your notes, and I was obsessed with their

shades and colors; their textures and

composition. Whether they were bright or

bittersweet, it didn't matter.

The strings of your soul were what

sustained me.

Without you, I was surrounded by silence.

The colorless, tone-deaf world I had been

living in had overwhelmed me.

But with you, I felt my own melody start to

compose itself.

So I sought you.

And each time I found you,

I came to life.

#

Your music is my heartbeat -

It gives my soul direction

EXCHANGE

Every word between us was magic.

When you met me in those dimly lit cafes
overlooking the city, I felt my heartbeat rush
through my ears like the street cars that
passed by, their drivers as clueless about my
feelings as you were.

You smiled as you sipped hot coffee,
speaking of your thoughts as if you trusted
me with them; as if you were giving me
permission to hold them for you while we
were away from each other.

The minutes passed into hours. Precious,
small hours that I treasured when I couldn't
see you. I wondered if you ever thought of
those moments as I did, if you ever smiled

when you heard my voice in your head.

On those days across the table, I felt like
someone else could see my soul and find it
beautiful. As if there were the possibility
that I could be the center of someone's
thoughts and heart; the possibility that
someone laid awake at night with dreams of
me beside them.

Maybe my words meant something.
Maybe my soul had some kind of melody of
its own.

There was nothing that made me feel more
beautiful than holding a hot drink in one
hand and holding your dreams in the other.

SHARP EYES

I had never seen such sharp eyes.

They curved like glass around your
eyelashes, reflecting the light and shadows;
holding both, and yet somehow, accepting
neither.

The whites were a strong contrast to the
haunted demons in your irises; stories of
good and evil within yourself cloaked in
mystery when you dropped your eyelids.

I saw heat when you stared at me, and I
wanted to feel it. I saw pain when you
looked at me, and I wanted to taste it.

And when you did nothing but glance, I felt
a cut between my logic and sanity. Your
eyes were blades that could cut my soul

from my body; the spinning needle that I
couldn't help but touch.

And when the light and darkness in your
eyes pricked my finger, I lost consciousness
to the world around me. There was only
you. For a moment, I could taste pain and
heat, good and evil, my soul and your body.

There was nothing more addicting than the
blood on my fingertips every time I touched
the forbidden spinning needle;
the demons leaving your eyes
to consume me,
the glass of your eyes blending us
into one reflection.

\#

You smiled differently as the night fell,

as if you and I were sharing a secret.

In exhausted pauses,

you rubbed your eyes...

and I wondered if I was the only one

who felt like I was dreaming.

MEET ME

Meet me in starlit alleyways
on those long, warm nights in June,
for pieces of broken conversation
I didn't realize I was craving.

In those awkward pauses,
I'll try to think of words
that will make me
more beautiful to you…

I want to be beautiful to you.

Even if that beauty
is full of silent uncertainties.

HE FINDS ME

He finds me where realities cease to be,
Between desires and melodies,
After dark, and deep in dreams.

He finds me where fear can't dwell,
Where trials and tribulations both have fell,
And our hearts know each other's well.

He finds me where we can't stay,
In a reality not existing in the day,
When morning comes, it all will fade.

He finds me only after dark, deep in
dreams,
Between desires and melodies,
Because we cannot exist in reality.

\#

I loved you as I loved the stars:

I looked up to you,

I made wishes on you,

And no matter what mountain I stood on,

I couldn't reach you.

INSOMNIA

You were my favorite form of insomnia.

Surrounded by darkness, I kept my eyes
open, wondering how many stars would fall
from the sky before you were lying next to
me. I imagined your lips... how they might
speak and tease when no one was watching;
their ratio of sugar and salt while expressing
desire in primordial ways. I imagined them
accompanied by the coarse curiosity of your
hands, positive they could conjure magic if I
could only get close enough.

In those moments, I would be able to see the
stars that had collected in your eyes,
hovering above me before crashing hard
against my self-control. Perhaps then I could
feel the elements of life: sharp breaths,

rushing blood, and the dizziness of freedom.

I didn't know what pleasures I could give
you, but I wanted to learn. I wanted to know
if I could cast the same spells as you. I
wanted to know my obsessions could be
returned in deliciously intimate ways that
people felt but never said aloud.

I wanted to be your insomnia.
I wanted you to taste the salt and sugar of
my obsession, until all you could see was
stars.

WEAVE

Tell me what dream I have to weave
to taste you,
what star I have to wish on
to feel your fingertips.

Lay me down in summer sun
to feel your heat,
and raise me up in winter moonlight
to feel your magic.

Drench me in stardust
so I can breathe you in,
let your glow seep into my skin
as you whisper dark secrets
for only me to hear.

Tell me how to tear a hole in the sky
and meet you where you are,

traveling the gaps between us.

Tell me what dream

I have to weave

to taste you,

tell me what star to wish on

to have you here.

\#

And for a short time,

you were intimately tucked away

from the world

next to my heart.

Only I could see you.

But I never knew

the world would eventually

reclaim you for its own.

MISDIRECT

I couldn't blame you for my misdirection. I could say that it was your fault that my soul wandered in dark directions, but it would be too transparent a lie. The truth is, I loved wandering. I loved exploring my fantasies of you and their endless possibilities. My obsession was better than my reality.

Both obsession and reality crushed me... but only obsession gave me the strength to stand again.

To you, it meant nothing. There was nothing in me that penetrated your heart the way that you did mine. I was nothing; a faceless shadow with starstruck eyes that you barely noticed in passing.

You were too bright to see me.

Everything in your circle was far too
illuminated.

And I…
I didn't know how to reach you.
I had wandered into too many dark
directions, unable to stand in your light.

CHAOTIC GRAVITY

I asked the stars to guide me to you
but all they did was spin in circles across the
sky; lost in chaotic gravity,
teasing me as they spun
but never landed.

They sparkled in a language
I couldn't understand,
keeping the pieces of your heart
that matched mine
a secret.

It's my fault.
The stars were jealous,
possessive,
knowing I'd abandon them
as soon as I could touch the light in your
eyes.

You were my star.

You were the light and fire I wished on

when the world turned dark.

The stars knew it.

So they separated us.

And so I was left with only chaotic gravity

pulling me into darkness,

my heart spinning

with no place to land.

FALL

Regardless of the circumstances, I fall.

Fall back into those patterns of restlessness,

recklessness,

unavoidable emotions

that I should have avoided

since the beginning.

I'm addicted to your cycle -

the way you breathe life into me as you

make me breathless,

the way my tears dry and drop

in your presence.

And you have no idea that you do it.

You have no idea how much I thirst for your

half-hearted attention, how I hunger for

your empty promises.

My soul numbed,
my body plagued with pins and needles
as I tried to wake up from my delusions.
But no matter how I wandered,
I couldn't make the blood flow
from fantasy to reality.

In this pain and pleasure, I'm yours.
Whichever fate you decide, I accept.

I'm too dizzy from these cycles to resist,
too reckless to take caution in your shadow.

REACH

I tried to reach you.

Through dreams, through prayers, through nights of wandering down empty streets, wondering which one led to you. But the streetlamps had gone out before I could find you, my prayers falling on the ears of a God who was jealous for my affections.

I saw you only in dreams; in fantastic scenarios conjured by a phantom who felt pity for my broken reality. My subconscious was merciful, weaving the strands of long forgotten memories into the sensation of your hands, lips, and heart.

I never knew how your possessiveness felt; I never knew the curve of your palm or the warmth of your fingertips, but my soul created them. Like an artist with a brush, it dipped in palettes of my imagination and created life.

My fingers could reach out and feel the feathery strands of your hair. My lips could trace the cut of your jaw and the smooth granite of your muscle. The wind transformed into your breath, and stone fruit from long ago summer days became your kiss.

I tasted hope in dreams, your scent and desire lingering behind my eyes until they opened.

And then, they faded. Reality swept them away with no remorse, satisfied with making me desire you even more.

But I couldn't reach you.
Not even God allowed it.

So I abandoned prayer to speak to you. I
began to look for something more powerful
than God to bring you to me.

#

I can't bring myself to wish on stars
anymore.
Not because wishes can't come true,
but because my wild dreams would take
the power of half the sky

SWEET

I sacrificed mundane possibilities for the grandiose fantasy you gave me. I could no longer sit in contentment when thinking of a normal daily life: a life of avoiding alarm clocks, selling off eight to ten pieces of my day for magic beans, and coming home to wash my hands and feet of it while I aged slowly in the mirror.

No, you added sugar to each dream, making it impossibly sweet and addicting. In my dreams, you promised a life of possibilities that children stopped believing in once all their teeth fell out. A place between Hollywood and Heaven, where contentment is found on open rooftops surrounded by stars.

And you were always the brightest star -
even before anyone else had ever seen you -
and I wanted that light for myself to fill in
my dark spaces.

In your light, the mundane would become
spectacular, rich colors coming out of
everyday life that I had never seen before.
Places of beauty and poetry that no one else
could see except us and the angels of God
who watched close in curiosity.

With you, I realized that our riches are
found in intimate conversation, while our
fame is found when we set our souls on fire
for all the world to see.

You lit the fire within me. And because of
you, I burned brighter than ever. I couldn't

imagine contentment in a life where that fire

turned back to embers.

I would have done anything

to keep burning.

EMPTY RELIGION

You changed me.

You uprooted every belief,
giving me a new, empty religion.
All my foundations were ruined,
desperate to find something to cement
the cracks deep within me.
You sold me the sand, but not the water;
and I was left thirsting as everything fell
through my fingers.

In your sun, my soul hardened.
My thoughts were too dry
to revive my blood,
and I became stone.
I only drank the saltwater of my tears,
and since you were the source,
I couldn't destroy you.

You were my only living water,

and if I didn't have you,

I wasn't sure I'd have anything at all.

It was better to thirst in misery

than to stop existing.

\#

The world finally saw your light,

the way I had always seen it.

And suddenly, my worship

was no longer enough.

I PRAYED I COULD LIE WITH YOU

I prayed I could lie with you

under the cherry blossoms

when winter had fallen

and my heart had awakened to spring.

Next to the river water,

the gloss of your eyes

captured in moonlight,

as you used every word you knew

to speak your soul into mine.

I prayed I could lie with you

so I could touch the shadows of your skin,

to leave marks on your neck

to tell the stars you were mine;

To taste salt from your skin

no one else had known,

and breath from your lungs

no one else had heard.

I prayed I could lie with you

so close that I could strip away

the collar of your shirt,

to see the heart hidden underneath.

I prayed I could lay my ear against

your hot chest to hear your heart beat,

pumping blood to every living cell

of your body

to remind me of how alive

we both were…

to remind me that God had allowed us both

to live until this moment.

I prayed I could lie with you

so that I could feel you

wrap me in your arms,

clutching me close to your soul

as you repeated your love for me,

over and over,

softer and softer,

until every angel heard it for themselves.

I prayed I could lie with you

to feel you kiss my fingertips

as I touched every edge and

every crack of your lips

until I knew your mouth

better than my own;

Until I knew your tongue -

its curves,

its taste,

its words -

better than my own breath.

I prayed I could lie with you

so for once

every sensation I knew of you

wasn't only a dream;

That you

for once

loved me as I loved you...

And that

for once -

for a moment -

for a breath in time -

you and I were one.

BESIDE YOU

I could admire you,

but I couldn't stand beside you…

and so I was left completely unsatisfied.

To be left only to worship but never be close

to you was a frustrating burden. Even God

made a bridge for His worshipers to cross,

but you never even handed me a rope.

I was far from you, but you were

comfortable with that. You had others

around you to block out the cold wind, and

I drifted with the breeze to the outer circles,

wondering how I was excommunicated

from your church so easily.

You knew I would worship you from a

distance. You knew I was loyal enough to

do it. So you took my love and praise and went where you pleased.

But I worshiped a god who only stole my energy and gave me no true reward for my dedication; a god who withheld love and blessing and comfort; a god no mortal could stand.

And I began to hate you. I hated the god you were to me - the god I worshiped - because you had turned your back on your faithful servant. You were an empty god who gave me nothing for my loyalty.

But I couldn't betray you.

And each day that I worshiped you
I began to hate you a little bit more.

\#

And so I've decided to stop loving you.

For the first time,

the second time,

the third

and the fourth…

But never - it seems -

for the last.

STEPS

And there were a thousand steps I needed to take to reach you, but there was no map to rely on. You took the stars from the sky so you could shine, and I was left with nothing to guide me.
No light.
No constellations.
Nothing to show me how to get to you.

You stood not as a guiding star, but as a blinding reflection of the sun.

With the sun and stars at your command, you had all the light you ever needed while I was surrounded by the cold darkness of a moonless night.

I was left to my own orbit - my own circles
to wander in - as gravity spun us apart even
further. We were part of the same galaxy,
but never part of the same sky.

We were star-crossed.

When you rose with the sun,
I could see everything reflected
in your light.

When I rose with the night,
you were asleep.

IRREPARABLE

I miss the way you once were, the way you
spoke, the cadence of your words when you
didn't want the world to hear us. I miss your
deep inflections, paired with slow
reflections; the way your intonation rose
and fell with my breath and self-control.

I was called a fool for loving you. And I
was.

And I am.

In my hopeless defense, your words were
full; carefully crafted in unwoven silk and
raw honesty. I could have torn my heart
from its reverence if lies had poured from
your lips, but, in fact, you meant every word
you spoke as if your heart couldn't hold

back its rhythm from your tongue.

And so I became enamored with your lips;
with every sound, every word... their
smooth curves and rough crevices. Your
sharp inhales and prolonged exhales
between heartbeats entranced me and
enslaved me until there was none of myself
left.

I was called obsessed. And I was.

And I am.

Then you saw your own words. You saw
their depth and sincerity, the value they
truly held. That must be why you hid them -
afraid an obsessed fool like me would
gamble them away. But how could I?

Your cadence, your inflection; your
intonation, your reflections made me who I
was. When your words broke, so did I.

And I was called irreparable.

And I was.

And I am.

\#

There are stars

I made wishes on

that I thought would never fall…

You were one of them.

DRIFTING

We started drifting.

You lowered yourself from divinity and became human; flawed and weak in places I hadn't inspected before. I never noticed the cracks in your jeweled crown, or the spider web of scratches on your glasses. I never saw the polish on your fake smile, nor the way you twisted your words into sweet nothingness when you spoke.

It wasn't that I loved you less. I couldn't.

But in seeing your flaws, I realized you had seen mine from the beginning. You never saw divinity in me. You never looked towards heaven to find me, because in your eyes, I was from the soiled earth. I was never the painted goddess of the moon I had hoped you would see me as - a light in the darkness for your heavy heart.

To you, I was just part of the darkness.

And somehow, we started drifting - you drifted from heaven, and I drifted from my belief in you.

I saw you flawless and I loved you.

You never saw me flawless
and that's why you loved someone else.

ENEMIES

I knew that one day we would become
enemies.

I knew that the glass case I built around you
to keep the dirt and chill out of your eyes
would eventually shatter, leaving me with
broken pieces that I cut my hands and feet.

There was nothing I could do to stop the
bleeding, and nothing pure enough to
cleanse the apathy out of your eyes.

I couldn't collect stardust and give it to you.
I couldn't collect your dreams and grant
them. If you had only told me how to reach
you, I would have done it.

But you never told me. And you never
asked how to reach my heart because you
never wanted it.

So I stopped trying to find the deepest, most
beautiful places of your soul - you had no
intentions to share them with me, anyways -
and I pretended I, too, didn't need you.

Only because it was less humiliating than
letting the world see
that I had loved you with everything I had.

LOVE AND OTHER BROKEN THINGS

One day I awoke to realize there was no you
and me. There had only been my one-sided
obsession, my declaration of love that had
never been returned.

My heart was a trinket on your shelf.
Nothing more. And so, the temple of glass I
had made to worship you shattered, the
shards dissolving into sand.

Those fragments – now turned to dust –
were everything I was made of:
My desires and my beliefs,
my heart, my soul, and dreams,
my light, my lust, my love,
and other broken things.

LEAVE

I didn't leave because I didn't love you.
There was nothing in me capable of that
kind of blasphemy; nothing in me able to
lack emotion when I looked at you. How
could I look at the deepest piece of myself
and hate it so? No... I could never stop
loving you.

You were the iron that sharpened my dull
spirit, pushing me until the shine returned
to my soul. When I looked in the mirror, I
saw you. When they asked me to spell out
my dreams, I wrote down your name.

Then... then a shadow passed over us, and
my blood wasn't enough to save us both.
They took your soul; they took the heart that
was synced with mine. They confused it,

they mutilated it, and they replaced it. They damaged you so you would look for the cure… then they became your god when they handed you the antidote.

Believing you owed them a debt for your salvation, you joyfully became their slave.

Now when I look in the mirror, it's empty. You had been so much of me. But now you are someone else, and I don't recognize either one of us.

I thought about chasing after you. I wanted to redeem you. But who was I to do it? I was nothing but your ghost… and how could you love something so empty?

No, I didn't leave because I didn't love you.

I loved you – I still love you – as the most

important part of me.

I left because I knew

there was no chance

of you loving me.

MERCY

There was no mercy for the weary.

There were nights I begged for you. Nights where the nightmare of reality stole all my dreams, to the point where hope felt like a luxury brand only affordable by the highest classes of society. I held tight to worn out blankets wrapped around my shoulders as pain leaked in through the windows; the cold bite of winter informing me that summer was just a passing season.

The worst pain was knowing that God could hear me; that He could see the pain that echoed in my skull every time it hit my pillow. He knew - no, He designed - my want and desire for you with no intention to deliver the promise. He built you the way that you were, knowing I would love you as much as I did... and in His stubborn morality to give mankind freewill, He allowed you to love someone else.

He gave you the happiness I had prayed for. He took my hopes and dreams and burnt them as incense, leaving me with nothing but soured memories and unanswered questions.

Suddenly love was a joke, like the Creator had created love just to show me how powerful and beautiful it was... but how a poor, broken soul like mine could never afford it. For me, love was only a window display.

God gave me the ability to love you…

but He refused to give you

the ability to treasure it.

In the end, I left God

just as you had left me,

as if it would teach Him

what this pain felt like.

PART TWO:

IDOLS, DEMONS, AND

MY OTHER CREATIONS

But each person is tempted when he is lured

and enticed by his own desire.

Then desire when it has conceived

gives birth to sin,

and sin when it is fully grown

brings forth death.

James 1:14

PATHS

And all the paths were open to me.

There was no you,
nor any other god to guilt me into purity.
I was free to take any path ahead since both
you and God had already abandoned me.

In turn, I abandoned you both.

And so in turn, I took the road
all three of us hated.

PROCESS

I don't know how to speak.

My thoughts don't wrap around emotion,

They don't process

positive or negative space.

I can only exist.

I am considered a failure to compassion,

to selflessness,

to awareness,

and that's why I use you.

When can't speak,

I imagine the taste

of the corners of your lips;

When my heart is cold

I imagine the heat of your hands.

In positive spaces, I use your light,

while the darkest corners hold your voice.

With you, I do not exist,

Instead, I live.

But in truth,

I have never been with you…

And that's why I am

compassionless,

selfish,

and unaware.

DARKNESS LIKE ME

It was the first time I had seen lust.

I had felt it in my own blood, unraveling the last pieces of myself worthy of Heaven. But you had never looked at me the way my heart looked at you. You had seen it in me, but this was the first time I had seen the darkness staring back at me, drowning me in a dangerous abyss.

Dark eyes sought me out and laid all its intentions on the table. It fanned out its cards - the king of hearts and the joker - giving me the option to hit or fold.

I knew he was playing a game... but you had never looked at me like that. You had never lost your breath next to me, unable to hide animalistic instincts.

After all, you were part of the stars. I was
part of the darkness. You would never fall to
grant my wishes.

So I threw my chips on the table, ready to
start an addiction I knew I would lose…
a sin that promised to destroy me.

It was better than hoping in your light;
A light that never sought me,
never saw me...
A light that only used
darkness like me to shine.

SHOULDN'T NOTICE

I shouldn't notice

the caramel of your skin

how each shadow

deepens

making you look sweeter,

the contours blending

angel and demon,

two creatures

I can't help but crave.

I shouldn't notice

the depth of your eyes

how their darkness

deepens

hiding your humanity,

locking away sin

and sorrow,

two pieces of your soul

I want to save.

I shouldn't notice

the shallow of your breath,

how each exhale

deepens

your lips parting to reveal

your words and groans,

two sounds

that give me life.

I shouldn't notice

how my obsession

deepens,

unhinging me from sanity,

tossing me between

angel and demon,

sin and sorrows,

words and groans,

until sin consumes my eyes.

LAND

I gave the devil a place to land.

He took off his coat, unafraid to show his true colors, knowing full well I had no disgust of them anymore.

He poured my darkness into a tall glass and left it for me on the table, the scent sweet despite its deadly colors. Thirsting to feel alive, I took it like a low-hanging fruit from the Garden, closing my eyes and bringing it to my lips.

It burned as I swallowed - a warning; but it was the only fire I had experienced in so long. My numbness subsided, and I saw my true colors.

I had seen God and I had seen the devil, but
I hadn't seen myself. I hadn't seen the
twisted pieces of my soul that ached for
control, nor the pure curves of my heart that
fought for redemption.

My purity had blockaded my path to
destruction,
but it had also caged me into a numb
existence.
My darkness promised to fill my senses…
and also, my complete annihilation.

And once I began to drink my darkness, I
couldn't stop. The desperation to feel every
ounce of myself again overwhelmed my
desire for redemption.

And the devil watched me as I drank, never

expecting my resistance, knowing what he

had known since his fall from the heavens:

that the dead always hand their souls over

to hell to live again.

#

And temptation took over

because I didn't have the strength

to love anymore.

I had never loved correctly

in the first place.

SILENCE

There was no music in him. That was the
commonality between us.

His words were plagiarized, a copy,
unoriginal. In truth, so were mine - all my
words were empty notes that I once took
from you.

When he drew near, I silenced him with sin.
I knew the moment his curved lips parted
they would only lie or - even worse - reveal
the truth.

My lungs were already filled with truth,
and that's why I was drowning.

So I begged for silence, for plagiarism, for
lies.

I wanted to forget

that I had no composition of my own.

#

I hated the pain.

Even more, I hated the pleasure.

But I endured it.

I endured pain

and pleasure

because it kept my mind off you….

an idol I couldn't stop worshiping.

It kept my mind off You…

a God who had stripped me of everything.

PURSUE ME

Pursue me.

Pursue me until there is nothing left of myself.

Relentlessly chase down hidden desires that I've failed to divide from my insecurities. Use your instincts to hunt down my dreams, until you can gaze into my heart and see all the stars I've wished on while thinking of your eyes.

Undress me with your lips; whispering words that break down all my defenses until I can do nothing else but surrender. Then wrap me in folds of silk as I trace the curves of your face, trapped by my own desire to taste the salt of the skin on your neck, and to

watch the way your ribs expand and retract
at my touch.

I am both entranced and imprisoned,
desperate and afraid - thirsting for
something that drowns my heart in painful
bliss, and yet starving for freedom from my
obsession. It's only fair that you are as
helpless as me.

So pursue me until you're as
consumed by me, as I am you;
until you're as idolatrous as I.

Pursue me.

Pursue me until there is nothing left of
yourself.

SALVATION

I became addicted to salt made in sin. The
way his shirt stuck to his lungs as he sucked
his breath in. As he lay beneath me, I broke
the fourth seal, killing my obedience and
sincerity towards both heaven and hell.

My dreams were the last of my contrition,
lain to ruin by angels who delivered
salvation by making sacrifices without my
permission. And demons offered me a
sponge of wine as I lay burning, laughing as
if I now belonged to them.

But it was the salt of his skin that saved me
from under heaven and hell's heel. Tight
fists wrapping around my pinching chains,
releasing me from the war I was drafted for;

the purgatory I was sentenced to for simply
existing.

And so I traded in my innocent dreams for
his salt, sweat, and breath...
for twisted revelation...
curious if the angels would sacrifice
that too
for my salvation.

\#

I turned away from the stars

knowing that my idol was still among them.

But it was impossible to hide from the light -

impossible to avoid the ache in my heart

at the thought of you shining above me.

FRAYED

I can only imagine nothing between us.

no space.

no words.

no apprehensions.

Slip your fingers over every ridge

of my spine,

weaving your strength into my vertebrae

as I grow weaker and weaker

for your lips;

the curves of your shoulders

keeping me from collapsing completely.

Swallow deeply as I pour my love into you,

desperate to escape the world in your kiss.

Let your tongue loosen and wander,

speaking and teasing

in possessive languages,

saving me from the edge

of my eternal emptiness.

Fill me up and mark me,

your constant heat

saving my heart from

freezing over completely,

your teeth and nails proving

that I'm not a pathetic fool lost to fantasy.

Soothe these jagged edges

with sharp breaths,

your fingerprints on my skin

proving my criminal dependency.

I'll gladly be imprisoned for my crimes

if it means being part of you.

I'll hang for my sins

since I can't stand without you.

I'll burn at the stake for my treason

since I can't live in Heaven anymore.

Pull me closer until there is nothing

between us.

no space.

no words.

no apprehensions.

Nothing but ragged breaths

matching the weary, frayed edges

of my heart.

#

I let the devil own me

because I had already mastered

enslaving myself.

It was someone else's turn.

ADDICTED

I was addicted to him

because of my addiction to you.

Had you been easy to forget,

easy to replace,

easy to remedy,

I would have never

looked for a replacement,

a secondary addiction to replace the first.

But when my lips touched his skin,

it was you.

When his arms held me close,

they were yours.

When he whispered in my ear,

it was your voice.

That voice that had saved me so long ago.

The voice I needed to own for myself...

The voice that compelled me
to sell my divinity.

I prayed to God to save me
while creating my own chains,
never meaning my prayers...
hoping for both my idol
and my salvation.

God rejected my prayers.
and you rejected my sin.

Knowing I couldn't own heaven -
neither God nor yours -
I created a living hell;
a way to feel something
on the descent
into insanity.

Even now in my delusion,

in my addiction,

in my hell,

I can't destroy you.

Even though the gold

I've wrapped you in

is crushing my soul.

Because if I lose my idol -

my ideal, my hope, my dream -

then I'm left with my reality:

a heart too condemned to be loved.

SATISFACTION

And I found satisfaction in my new idolatry.

It had been the same when I loved you, so long ago, before the stars took you as one of their own.

I was in love with your light until I was so blinded by you that I could no longer see God. I didn't want Him. I only wanted His ability to give you to me.

Home was never promised to me, never offered. God wanted me homeless, empty, and wandering; separated from the stars for His own glory.

I didn't belong to you, so I didn't want to belong to Him.

I filled myself with sin and pleasure to spite
you both. I filled myself with pain because it
was the closest sensation to loving you.

Yes, the darkness was heavy…
but I was hollow
and it was the only thing that could fill me.

I had worshiped light only to lose my
salvation, and so I gave myself over to
darkness to gain hell.

At least now I owned something eternal.

SALTWATER

Saltwater rushing over my lips, reminding me of the taste of your skin. I slip deeper and deeper into black water, light on the surface reflecting the Heaven I turned away for sin.

Disrupted dreams - my conscience suddenly unconscious when I close my eyes and see your face. You were the creator of temptation… and I could not resist worshiping you, awake or asleep.

As dark strands of soft sin fall across your eyes, allow me to get lost in the curve of your lips that whisper pure words I plan to taint with darkness.

If you truly love me, I'll never know.

I'd rather own your shadows,

knowing I can never own my own light.

\#

It was not love

that destroyed me

but greed.

My love was too weak

to do anything valuable.

JEWELS

Everything became empty.

They offered me jewels but I had no interest;
not because I was humble or great, but
because I knew my demons couldn't be fed
diamonds. They had blurred my sight until I
no longer saw beauty. They broke my walls
and mirrors, and the shards of glass that
once showed a clear reflection now dug into
my eyes and destroyed my vision… turning
everything into pure hell.

I no longer saw you. Maybe I never had. But
now I saw myself - my true self - in those
painful shards buried too deep for
reflection.

I was the demon that couldn't be fed diamonds. I was the guilty, the ashamed, the selfish, and the offender.

I had destroyed myself by first degree murder, knowing that the way I loved you would be the death of me.

Even with these cuts in my eyes, you were beautiful. And you would have stayed that way if I had never reached out to take you for myself. But when my fingers touched your skin, the merciless shards in my eyes showed me how I had ruined you.

I made you empty.

And in turn, the world became empty to reflect you.

REVERSE OBSESSION

And I lived in a reverse obsession.

I licked both the salt and the wound, the sting on my tongue and cuts a mild distraction from you.

There was nothing more bitter than blood I had let in order to cure myself of my self-inflicted disease.

I had traded innocence for idolatry, idolatry for religion, only to realize it was devil worship.

Confusing you for the sun, I flew into your light until my wings melted, condemning myself to the status of a fallen angel by my own greed to shine.

You warned me of my blind spots, but instead of heeding your advice, I shut my eyes until there was only darkness.

That was all that was left within me.

But even in hell I hoped in you, refusing to give you up as my god. You never asked for the position - and even begged I didn't crown you - but I needed a god so badly that I forced you into a coronation and contract, one where I damned my own soul in exchange to worship you.

And when you threw down your crown in anguish and fled, I cared less about your pain and more that I had no one to worship.

And so I lived in reverse obsession...

Doing anything I could to forget you...

Filling the void of worship with pain

because it was what I deserved for my sins.

#

And I started to realize

who I was

and who I wasn't,

Who you were

and who I had made you to be.

You were made of

starlight and melodies,

while I was only

darkness and broken plagiarism.

And there was nothing to save me.

I had abandoned all of my saviors.

PEDESTAL

I've created an obsession
a hollow love -
a monster made from rejection -
a pedestal for someone who never truly
earned it.
I've created an obsession
with myself.

That pedestal, I made for you
and you climbed on it easily
breathlessly
because I tore off my wings
and gave them to you consciously.

But in the end,
you stepped off the pedestal I made
and handed them back to me,
Your knees as broken as my wings

from holding up the weight I put on you -

from holding up all my dreams.

So I climbed on the pedestal myself

with broken wings that couldn't fly

standing too close to my own sun,

and demanded my own part of the sky.

And the longer I stood

the more they burned

until they turned dark,

beyond any healing.

But I couldn't come down from the pedestal,

you see,

because I finally was on top.

I was no longer small, looking up to you

for validation

I was now the fabrication of all my dreams.

But...

On my pedestal, I could only stare at my
own reflection,
It's shine now my only validation
And I created my monster -
my obsession -
because I couldn't handle any more
rejection.
So I sat on my pedestal -
alone -
because pedestals are not made for two -
and I wrote word after word
and yelled out a few
hoping someone could hear my heart
because it felt like no one knew.

And I took shot after shot
of myself from all angles

to admire my own beauty

to prove that it exists, that I'm able

to be loved.

But only when I looked down

could I see my true self:

The empty, hollow

beauty of myself

reflected in this pedestal I made.

PART THREE:

GOD, THE SEA,

AND OTHER MEDICATIONS

The cure for anything is salt water —

sweat, tears, or the sea.

— Isak Dinesen

\#

I became the waves.

Repetitive.

Cold and crashing constantly.

Tossing and turning.

My soul begging for the shore,

My heart crying out for a lighthouse.

Without you, there was no me.

Without You there couldn't be.

GONE

Then you were gone.

I felt you separate from my soul,
severed by our purposes. They were not
meant to cross, to fuse, to stand together.
They were only meant to coexist,
one standing on the east side
and one on the west.

And when our souls separated, I saw the
frayed threads that had weaved them
together. I saw my own lack of care, for both
your strands and mine. I had been too
absorbed in weaving us together to notice
the poor quality of the final product.

I wanted a beautiful tapestry to call mine.

And I couldn't think of anything more beautiful than you.

But the tapestry tore - from bottom to top - unveiling my poor craftsmanship and the truth of our union. We couldn't hold together. Not with my craftsmanship.

I couldn't even craft myself.

Because the threads of my soul were frail and ill-conditioned, they couldn't be joined with yours. You were made of the highest quality. I was made of the poorest yarn.

Therefore, anything weaved with my soul was bound to disintegrate.

THREADS

Eventually there was no escape
from myself.

I was forced to unbutton my skin and look
underneath; tasked to look at every thread,
at the mess I had made.

I tore them out and held them in my fingers
in grief, realizing they were only poor
imitations of you. Your beauty was beyond
mine. It was my greatest torture; I spent my
time either loving you or wanting to become
you.

But I couldn't love you.
And I couldn't become you.
And I didn't know how to become myself.

I could see beauty in everything except myself.

So I tore out every thread until I was naked, mixing the strands of myself with my tears, begging to be made into something beautiful with frayed, weak threads.

\#

I teetered on the edge of ocean cliffs

half entranced by the beauty before me,

half tempted to step off the side.

THEN CAME AUTUMN

When summer faded, the world rejoiced.
The crowds spoke of the beauty of autumn,
and the soothing winds to come. Wrapped
in warm jackets, they sang as the leaves fell.

But I stood on the horizon, looking back
towards the sun, begging him not to go.
There was nothing else that could warm me,
nothing else to bring me light.

I had lost you.
I had lost God.
I had lost myself.
And to lose the sun
would be the last of my power.

As the crowds wrapped their jackets around
themselves, I sought comfort. As they

embraced the wind, it blew straight through my empty soul. And when they sang of beauty, I knew there were no songs with my name in it.

When autumn came,
the leaves slowly began to die.

So did I.

SWALLOWED

Swallowed by my greed

for a future

not meant to be mine,

Stumbling through a maze

that traps my clouded mind,

I touch the walls

and come back with burns

but I can't get

get myself to leave,

because

better to be spurned

by a future fantasy

than admit that

in the present

I'm nobody,

someone who's lost all control,

a degrading body

with an aching soul.

Regardless

they all pat me on the back,

as I cross the finish line

they clap -

they cheer as I shine

while I pop another pill

wondering if I'll ever be fine.

They tell me I leave

such a good impression

as I lay silent

in my oppression

a slave to the masters of my time.

Down to my bones

my smile hangs off my skin

holding on in desperation

as fear shuts down my respiration,

choking on the poison

I forced myself to drink

swallowing toxic thoughts

I trained myself to think,

playing with the rusted knives

I thought would cut my chains

but instead helped me further bleed.

Can I ever meet my dreams?

even if they weren't meant for me?

Constantly choosing between

my passion and my peace,

losing them both

to my anxieties,

wondering if I'll ever soar

when I'm grounded by hospital IVs.

Can I reach my full heights

when I dig my own grave

with an empty life?

Will I reach that potential,

that life that fulfills my need

to be influential…

so I know I didn't waste my breath.

I plant seeds, but

nothing grows from where I bled,

nothing's harvested as I sweat

and the skies taunt me overhead,

knowing my heart is completely dead,

that my dreams would never see the light

and instead…

I'd be swallowed whole by the night

knowing my idol,

my God,

and my sanity

all have turned their backs on me,

because I turned on them first

when I realized I couldn't

love them properly.

\#

They asked me to walk on water

but I didn't even have strength

to come to my knees.

BLOWING WIND

On the winter path, I looked for you still.

I had no interest in a single pair of
footprints; it made the road too long and the
stars too distant. And though the snow and
wind ripped my soul to pieces, I wandered
any path I could find to reach you.

I had abandoned darkness just as quickly as
I had abandoned the light.
Now I had neither.

And since there were no stars - no you - I
couldn't follow them. In mercy, the wind
blew in circles until I followed.

The only warmth was in the sunset, a
reminder that each day ended, that each

season ended, that pain – too – would set
with the sky. And I held onto this as each
one of my footsteps became colder than the
last. I walked parallel to your shadow,
wondering if our paths would ever cross
again.

Regardless of its chill, the wind whispered
its hope to me. It had gone from one edge of
the world to the next; and as I walked
parallel to your shadow, the wind told me of
what was yet to be.

No more shadows, but light.
No more sunsets, but rises.
No more winter, but spring.

And when it was done speaking, your
shadow steered left from mine. I knew the

only way our paths would cross would be if the wind turned you around... but the wind only blew in circles around me. Not you.

You knew your path and followed. The wind now had to convince me to take my own.

And with dreams of spring... I followed.

\#

Our conversations were always

my most precious treasure.

It's a shame they were all imaginary.

SEE THE SNOW

I wish that I could see the snow

in its purest, cleanest glow;

Where all is dead, drenched in white,

sweet peace from harsh seasons -

time's afterlife.

For deep underground is a new birth,

waiting to overcome winter's current world,

and I wish there was snow

outside to assure me

that beautiful things will come to be.

But here I am, surrounded by the spring -

hope has been born,

and new songs now ring -

But my song has not changed,

and there's nothing to say

that hope for my world is on its way.

LIGHTS

There were lights in the distance I couldn't own.

I saw them frequently, counting them like stars and wondering if they were lost to the sky also. There were days I was brave enough to search them out, but they only disappeared as I got closer, not ready to reveal themselves to me, never wanting me to own them.

The people in the cities told me not to look for them.

"Look at all the jewels we have in our kingdom!" they said. "Why would you be interested in those lights in the distance?"

Then they handed me the jewels they spoke
of, bragging of their fine quality. But as I
held them, I realized they were made of
flawed glass; fragile and easily shattered.

Oh! but they had become so precious to the
people in the cities, and they replaced their
brick walls with glass jewels, chattering
more about glass ceilings than of walls that
would never withstand a storm.

And I was considered a fool for wanting
those lights in the distance, fodder for the
gossip mills who couldn't understand why I
had no interest in glass ceilings.

I was only interested in the stars beyond
them.

I wanted those faint lights in the distance
that no one ever looked at, blinded by the
light of their fragile glass jewels.

They never realized that glass
was easily blown back to sand,
while the stars were made of fire.

And so I continued to search for the lights in
the distance, praying I could own a fire so
bright that I could never be blown back into
dust.

\#

I had nothing to offer.

Maybe that's why

I tried to strip you

of everything you were.

MORNING STAR

In agony, I followed the morning star.

I hadn't realized that there were two of
them: one made of darkness and the other of
light. They blended together so I couldn't
not decipher them, so I could not tell one
voice from the other.

And so I followed whichever voice suited
me in the moment, whichever voice filled
the holes that so desperately needed
fulfillment.

I was too weak to lean into the Morning Star
of Light that told me to endure; that
promised to heal me once the pain had run
its course.

So I, instead, swallowed the toxins of the Morning Star of Darkness, who promised to numb the pain for the day.

I followed both morning stars until there was a fork in the road... until I had to choose which one to follow.

I knew the Morning Star of Darkness was an empty imitation; a false light designed to burn me in the end. But who was I to follow the Morning Star of Light? I had already abandoned Him and had no strength to return.

So I sat on the fork of the road - between the Morning Star of Light and the Morning Star of Darkness - knowing I would possess my heart's full desires if I only walked right.

But I was unable to step forward because I didn't know how I could ever deserve them.

\#

As I stood on the shore

I waited for only the largest waves,

stepping out to meet them

as they overwhelmed me.

I didn't want to die.

I was just tired of losing.

I wanted to know what it felt like

to face something great

and withstand it.

.

HOLES

It took me until now to see the holes: the disconnected pieces of my heart and soul that created the formless body reflected in my mirror.

I never acknowledged them. Instead, I filled my heart and soul with you, attempting to seal the dead spaces.

And when you proved not to be the glue I needed to hold myself together, I reinvented you. I erased your true composition and started over.

I wanted your voice to repair those empty spaces. I wanted your lips to hold me together.

But you could not be composed of two people. You couldn't merge your voice with my empty spaces. You couldn't cure my pain... I didn't even allow you to express your own.

And so I destroyed us both. I knew it, but I didn't stop... because who I wasn't was more important to me than who you were.

And so in truth,
neither one of us truly existed.

#

I loved you

not because I valued you,

but because I valued the things

I had felt for the first time.

SPUN

Fears spun my head and my heels, turning me around the city to wander crowded streets to find you. I met with the eyes of every pedestrian, trying to find you once more... losing the sense of direction in both my feet and my soul. I ached to reach you, but God decided our paths were not to cross no matter how many steps I took.

When I closed my eyes, I felt your soul next to mine; searching as much as I was.

I prayed for messengers, for angels, for affirmation. I walked snow-covered hills until my toes were numb. I walked down overflowing streets until my knees were weak. And when I dreamed, I searched for you there until I woke.

But even in my dreams, you turned away
when you saw me.

I knew there was no bargain I could make
with God - the God I had abandoned for
you - because I didn't even deserve the
grace He had given me to begin with. And I
turned away from His comfort not because I
hated Him, but because my soul felt too
much guilt to accept forgiveness.

I had ruined you,
both in reality and in dreams.

And so my soul twisted in fear
while I was both asleep and awake,
wondering if my wrong steps
had cost me everything.

DIVINITY

Laying on the sand, I pray to the stars to tell me how to reach you. Not the you I knew, but the ideal I had created.

That dream that I hid in the most selfish parts of my spirit that could never accept reality for what it was.

You were the personification of my hope; a god formed by an unholy desire to have everything. I placed you higher than the stars and brighter than the moon... not understanding that in that light, I would never find warmth.

And you knew my delusion and idolatry, warning me that you were not the god I had painted you as. But I refused the red skies and sailed into my worship. I felt the wind in my hair and the thrill of the waves underneath me, ignoring the storm on the horizon.

In that storm, my sails tore and my ship shattered. I found in the rubble the beautiful, pure pieces of you that I had never seen before; your true self that you were trying to show me. That beautiful creature was trapped in the idol I had made... and when I found him, it was too late.

If I had only seen you as a man instead of a god... then I would have found satisfaction in your humanity and not disappointment in your divinity.

\#

And when I looked up,

God burned promises into the sky…

Not because I deserved them,

but to show me that He

was the only One powerful enough

to grant the wishes I had made.

UNDESERVING

God made me promises I couldn't keep.

He offered me stars but I couldn't hold
them; not with my hands as stained as they
were. I had nothing to offer as a trade, my
soul tainted and destroyed beyond my own
recognition.

How could God know me
when there was nothing left?

My soul collapsed next to the living well,
too guilty to take a drink. The stars above
me whispered peace undeserving, offering a
path if I only I drank and then stood to
follow.

I told them I was guilty, and they agreed. I

told them I was worthless, and they were silent. I told them I was hopeless, and they shot across the sky.

But there were no wishes I could deserve. After all, God didn't bless demons. He didn't spare angels fallen from grace. And I - who was no better than a fallen angel - couldn't bring myself to hope.

I could only beg.

Beg for hope though I was wishless. Beg for forgiveness when I was guilty. Beg for value when I was worthless.

And beg that God would keep the promises I didn't deserve.

HE TELLS ME

He tells me to wait

when waters rise,

strong ebb and flow

is part of the tide.

Whether it's too deep

or completely dry,

He's always in control.

He tells me to rest

when the sun has fell,

to look up when fear

traps me in a spell.

He sends stars because

He knows darkness well,

along with weary pieces of my soul.

He tells me to walk

when the path is steep,

when it's hard to climb,

when it's hard to breathe,

because through it all

He won't abandon me -

When I'm weak,

my God makes me whole.

REFLECTIONS

When I looked down in the water,

I saw the who I wanted to be.

I saw the reflection of the sky,

a vessel which held

up darkness and the night,

and yet,

a surface that reflected beauty

with pure and blinding light.

And whoever gazed upon the water

felt peace and holy yearning,

whoever stood next to it

felt their strength slowly returning,

and whoever drank from it

felt full with no thirst nagging at their soul.

As I looked…

and looked…

and looked…

at that reflection,

I longed to be someone who could

stand in darkness,

in death

in fire

in resurrection…

A messenger of day and night;

pure, blinding beauty

that could hold

and reflect

the Light.

\#

And the waves cleansed the broken glass.

The salt of my tears
stripped away everything
I had once been.

I was still shattered,
but I was now transparent.

And the stars reflecting
in the shards at my feet
encouraged me to hope again.

MOSAIC

I quit searching for someone to put me together.

The shards of my heart, soul, and mind were too shattered to glue together, beyond any repair of this world.

So I left all the pieces on the altar, knowing that my hands couldn't fix them. Nothing could. Not you, not addiction, not myself.

And when God looked at the shattered pieces I had given Him on the altar, He told me that He wouldn't restore them to their original design.

He then collected my words as they turned into tears, mixing them with the sands of time to create thicker glass. He scattered the shattered pieces of my heart, soul, and mind in a frame; sealing it before taking His work firmly by the frame and hanging it in the window.

I had become a mosaic.

And for the first time,
I now reflected the light.

COMPOSITION

Yes, I was deeply in love with your voice.

I was lost in your rich tones, the dark and
sweet curves in your voice and your artistry,
and the way it connected with the most
hidden pieces of me. I never knew my own
depths until the vibrations of your voice
brought them to the surface.

I never asked who I was until you asked me.
I never asked who I was until I wanted you
to know me.

I never even considered my own
composition, not until I realized the
melodies and metaphors that created you.
Your heart held the power of the sea, your
mind held the clarity of starlit skies. Your

smile was made of innocence and sin; your touch made of warm, fragile memories. The barest, purest elements combined to create the one and only you - never to combine into something so breathtaking again.

But women like me - women who see men like you made of stardust and artistry - we're not allowed to speak of such things. We're called desperate and dependent, foolish and old-fashioned, nothing but the uncivilized lost in dreams.

So as I fell deeper and deeper into your composition, I told no one. I kept you my wonderful secret, refusing to allow anyone to see how I loved you. I didn't let anyone see the light I had you in.

And eventually that light that I had on you reflected onto me. For the first time I saw my own composition... realizing my own melodies and metaphors, my own depths and purities.

I never saw who I was until I saw you.
I never loved who I was until I loved you.

I never saw who I was until I saw You.
I never loved who I was until I loved You.

And so
because of you,
and because of You,
I became a new composition.

AUTHOR'S NOTE

These are my most devastating confessions.

Originally, I only wanted to put my poems into a small collection for my own keeping, but my inner storyteller saw the storyline of my own experience and urged me to write down the full journey.

The narrator begins with an infatuation that turns into an idolatrous obsession; causing her to hate both her earthly idol and God when neither seem concerned for her affections.

She then turns to the addiction of fantasy to numb the pain, only to end up destroying herself even more.

And finally, realizing that she now has

nothing - and deserves nothing - she returns to her God, defeated. She becomes a new person because of both her idol - whom she now can see as a man instead of as a god - and God Himself, who had been waiting to form her into a vessel of light since the beginning.

This was painful for me to write. This was not a story, but an autobiography. These pages are full of raw emotions that still sting when poked.

I've always believed that to love someone and have them not love you in return is the greatest pain of all; and it was designed that way because I can't think of a greater pain to

God than when we turn away from Him when He offers His love to us.

I cannot say that the wounds completely heal after finding God, or that love suddenly works favorably; but at least in that love, I have something that moves me forward when everything seems broken. God has made it His occupation to restore, rebuild, and renew.

He writes every human composition.

Every struggle, every pain, every fear become notes.

Every hope and dream become a chord.

The beating of our hearts becomes a rhythm.

Those who cross our paths become the
accompaniment.

And before we know it, we are composed.
And recomposed.
And rewritten.
Until we become symphonies.

May you never give up on the journey until
you've seen your own symphony,
your own composition;
until you see that broken things
still reflect the light.

- Deidrea Dewitt

OTHER WORKS BY DEIDREA DEWITT

CHOOSE THE ENDING SERIES

The Five Princes

The Rebellion

SHORT STORIES

The Exchange

ABOUT THE AUTHOR

Deidrea is a California native who currently
lives in South Korea as an author, teacher,
and philosophy/theology major.

She is the author of the CHOOSE THE
ENDING series, the romance series that lets
YOU choose how the story ends.

Her greatest loves include classic and Gothic
literature, the struggle of good and evil in
the human soul, and pancakes.